W9-AVC-716

How Do I Feel?

I FEEL MAD

By Katie Kawa

Please visit our website, www.garethstevens.com. For a free color catalog of all our high-quality books, call toll free 1-800-542-2595 or fax 1-877-542-2596.

Library of Congress Cataloging-in-Publication Data

Kawa, Katie.
I feel mad / Katie Kawa.
p. cm. — (How do I feel?)
Includes index.
ISBN 978-1-4339-8116-6 (pbk.)
ISBN 978-1-4339-8117-3 (6-pack)
ISBN 978-1-4339-8115-9 (library binding)
1. Anger in children—Juvenile literature. I. Title.
BF723.A4K39 2013
152.4'7—dc23

2012019213

First Edition

Published in 2013 by
Gareth Stevens Publishing
111 East 14th Street, Suite 349
New York, NY 10003

Editor: Katie Kawa
Designer: Mickey Harmon

Printed in the United States of America

CPSIA compliance information: Batch #CW13GS: For further information contact Gareth Stevens, New York, New York at 1-800-542-2595.

Contents

I like to play
with my toy car
after school.
It is a red car.

It has four black wheels.

My big brother likes
to hide my car.
His name is Matt.

Matt hides my car
under his bed.

I do not like
when Matt hides my car.
It makes me feel mad.

I yell at Matt
when I am mad at him.

Matt says he is sorry
for hiding my car.
This is called
an apology.

I say I am sorry
for yelling at Matt.

I am not mad
at Matt anymore.
I give him a hug.

Then, we play
with my car together.

Words to Know

brother

wheels

Index